Audition

Anne Eton

This paperback is also available as an ebook at most online ebook retailers.

Copyright 2014 Beginnings Press

ISBN-13: 978-1-62602-038-2

ISBN-10: 1626020388

Deborah Rothstein studied her quarry.

She and her guest were sitting at a small patio table at the Ivy. The restaurant was one of the most prestigious watering holes in the industry. "The industry," of course, meaning the entertainment business in Los Angeles.

Deborah had come far, fast. After graduating from New York University a mere three years previously, she had moved to the West Coast and attained a position as a junior agent in one of the industry's most powerful agencies. When she had attended NYU Deborah had initially studied acting. But she had soon switched her focus to the business aspect of film. It played to her natural strengths. A student movie she had produced her senior year had almost won an Academy Award for Best Short Film.

But that didn't cut any ice in the industry, and Deborah knew it. So her plan was to work her way up to full agent, make lots of contacts among A-list actors, and perhaps even "break" one or two (help them be discovered) so as to indebt them to her. She would then shift into producing. Deborah was determined to be the next Sam Spiegel, the legendary producer of *The African Queen*, *Lawrence of Arabia* and many other classic films. Everyone who knew Deborah agreed that it was certainly possible.

After beginning her career in her agency's mailroom, Deborah had flirted and traded and backstabbed her way into a small office with her own assistant. Three years had been a long time, for her. Junior agent would not cut it. She needed to become full agent. But the only way that would happen soon was if one of her acting clients landed a lead role in a studio movie.

And that was how Deborah had come to be having lunch that day at the Ivy with the fortysomething Houda Al-Anselemmy.

Houda was Egyptian. But she never actually spent much time in Egypt. She instead shuttled between mansions in London and New York and Gstaad. Her family was extremely wealthy. Houda's great-great-grandfather had made a fortune in Egyptian cotton plantations; his descendants had expanded and diversified the family's holdings. However, Houda's father had died when she had been very young. She had been his only child. And so Houda had become the sole heir to an empire that included cotton, rubber, shipping, and incidentally London's biggest and most famous department store.

Upon turning twenty-one Houda had begun expanding her family's holdings, ruthlessly selling and acquiring companies. In the process she became internationally respected and feared. She was invariably the cover girl on any business magazine's feature story about female titans of industry. But by Houda's own admission, business had never really excited her. Movies on the other hand had always fascinated her. That's what she had said, anyway, in a short interview. She had been quoted by the industry daily *The Hollywood Reporter* after having arrived in Los Angeles six months previously.

Deborah had read the interview over and over, trying to glean any kind of a hint into this staggeringly wealthy woman's mind. The article had been on the occasion of a major studio's announcement that it had entered into a co-production agreement with Houda's newly formed film company. The studio had given Houda a producer's cottage on the lot. She, and only she, would greenlight three films in the studio's so-called "independent" division that year. Basically, Houda had bought her way in, though of course the *HR* story did not put it so crassly. But everyone understood.

The Egyptian woman had immediately been besieged by every agent in Hollywood. Reps wanted to pitch their actors, directors, et cetera.

But Houda had accepted no meetings; her assistant always answered her phone, and only ever said, "Send us some headshots."

And the agencies did—literally tons of US mail. (No one knew Houda's email address.)

Yet still Houda had not replied to anyone—no calls, no meetings, no appearances at industry parties. It was very peculiar. And it wasn't like an agent could get to Houda's husband or boyfriend, because she didn't have one. She had never had one. Interesting.

Using her typical shrewdness, Deborah Rothstein had decided to take a different approach with Houda. She had mailed Houda only one headshot—of herself. The full-body black-and-white photo had been taken back during Deborah's freshman acting days at NYU. It showed Deborah in her underwear, bent over a dresser and looking over her shoulder at the photographer with a saucy smile. The photo had been publicity for a play about repressed housewives or something—Deborah did not quite remember. But she figured that she, Deborah, had something that other much more powerful agents did not: a young hot body. Deborah Rothstein knew that she was no Scarlett Johansson; more like an ingénue Bette Midler with a frizzy brown Jewfro and a tight ass. She had had no idea if her ploy would work. But hey, she had nothing to lose. On the photo she had written: *"Houda, it takes an actor to know actors. Prior to agenting I was a thespian in college! I would love to talk to you about my actor clients and opportunities for our mutual benefit. Most sincerely, Debbie."*

Houda's office had called within a week. Would Ms. Rothstein be available for lunch at the Ivy?

Would Ms. Rothstein be available!

Deborah had learned everything she could about Houda prior to the lunch date. Houda was in her forties. Early years in elite boarding schools had trained her poise. Her manners were flawless. She also looked striking. People said she had a personal trainer and an intense fitness regimen. Her dark face was not conventionally attractive; but her smoky eyes, sharp cheekbones and sly knowing smile gave her a dangerously sexy quality. The woman radiated power. She had been catered to all of her life. She expected nothing less.

Deborah was ready to reel in a very big fish.

But now, here at the Ivy, the junior agent found her big plans circling the drain. Try as she might, Deborah could not hold Houda's attention. The Egyptian woman's perfectly-coiffed head would turn at the approach of any pretty girl among the pedestrian traffic next to them; Deborah had paid off the maître d' in advance to seat them next to the sidewalk. She had wanted to show off to any industry passerby that she, Debbie Rothstein, had landed a lunch with Houda.

Big mistake. Houda only seemed interested in the pretty girls.

After an hour of sales-pitching to no avail, Deborah stopped talking. She tried to think. *What's it gonna take? Houda's not interested in YOU so you can't leverage what's under your clothes. Why then did she want to have lunch with you? Shit, none of this makes sense. Aaaaarghh…*

Calm down, Debbie. Concentrate.

Okay. Houda's producing three movies and it's not bullshit, your sources confirmed from accountants at the studio that money is already being spent on pre-production. But no one's been cast. Yet. And as far as you know, no agent's gotten this close to Houda before.

If Houda wanted A-list talent she'd be having lunch with someone else. So she doesn't want A-list talent. Then what DOES she want? She set up this lunch after you sent her a picture of yourself where you looked a stripper. But—

At that moment, as if in a kismet of psychic connection, Houda turned to Deborah with a sexy smile. Her dark eyes were gleaming. She had been studying a very blonde, very fit, very innocent-looking chick in a white dress who had been wandering down the street with a water bottle in hand.

Houda leaned over the table and whispered to Deborah in a throaty upper-class English accent: "If one wished to start a strip club, the best recruits would all be here!" She laughed and fluttered her hand at the sidewalk.

That's it, Deborah thought. Her head whipped around as she studied the blonde sashaying away. Houda seemed to have been particularly excited by her. *Well, well, well. Finally, something I can work with.*

"You know," Deborah said casually, drawing on her acting training so that her excitement would not tinge her voice. "I have clients who look exactly... like... her." She dipped her head at the disappearing blonde before taking a small sip of water from a chilled crystal tumbler.

The Egyptian heiress slowly turned. For the first time, Debbie had Houda's complete attention.

Back at the agency, Debbie ran into her office as she shouted at her assistant: "I need blondes, blondes, blondes! Lots of them! And redheads! We're going to be here all night! Go to the mailroom and get everything in the slush pile, every goddamn headshot from every actress-model-whatever!"

As she leaped into her office chair, Debbie tried to organize her thoughts. She had a lot of work to do. Her boast to Houda had been a lie, of course: the junior agent did not really have any clients who looked like the girl on the sidewalk. But hey. That was an easy fix.

* * *

Jenny Smith walked across the downtown

Burbank street toward massive film studio gates. She tried to remember everything her new agent had told her. The past week had been quite a whirlwind.

The young blonde actress had arrived in Los Angeles a month ago from a tiny town in Kansas. She was determined to make a career for herself in the movies. True, she did not have much experience, but that was to be expected—she had only just graduated from high school. Upon arrival in L.A. she had sent out resumes and headshots to every talent agency in town, and meanwhile had found work as a barista.

Initially she had been disappointed that none of the agencies had contacted her. But then suddenly, just one week ago, an agency had called. Her coffeehouse co-workers had told her subsequently, in hushed tones, that it in fact was the most powerful talent agency in Hollywood. Jenny had been thrilled but not really surprised. Lots of crazy things had happened in her life. It was like her life was destined by fate!

The agent, Deborah, had insisted that Jenny come in that same day. So Jenny had found someone to cover her shift. She asked a favor of a male coworker who had seemed smitten with Jenny's blonde curvy all-American good looks. The guy had asked jokingly if she had landed an audition for a Barbie commercial. Jenny didn't like him. She didn't like most men.

At the agency, Deborah had appeared

exhausted. The junior agent had had bags under her eyes. Her first words had been, "You need to lose the glasses."

"My glasses?" Jenny had touched the gigantic plastic frames with an uncertain finger. "But they are really hip. They're what all the basketball players are wearing…"

"Get contacts. Today. And you'll need to go shopping."

In five minutes flat Jenny had taken notes on a white Macy's dress that Deborah had shown her on the internet. Deborah had made Jenny write down the catalog number.

"So you're going to go to Macy's *today* and buy that dress, right?"

"Yes, well, okay," Jenny had said a little breathlessly. "But what is this all about?"

"Look, there isn't much time. I'll tell you tomorrow. Opportunity is knocking. We may not get another chance. And I do mean we. I need to know how committed you are. Do you want to sign with me, or not?"

"I do, I do!"

"Good, I want you to sign with me too. Now listen carefully. Tomorrow, wear the dress. Go to this hair salon, eight a.m." Deborah had handed Jenny a business card. "I've already talked to Miguel. He's the best. He's going to give you an amazing hairstyle. I guarantee it will look sexy."

"My *hair?*" Jenny had run her fingers through her long blonde locks. True, she did have a curled-bang look in front that was a little geeky, but she thought it looked hip and retro.

"Miguel's not cheap," Deborah had said. "But you've got a credit card, right? This is an investment. Then I want you to go immediately after that to this other guy." Deborah had handed the dazed girl another business card. "His studio is on Pico. He will give you the most amazing headshots that anybody has ever seen."

"How much is all this going to cost me?"

"I don't know."

Jenny had thought hard. Deborah had waited.

"Okay," Jenny had said finally. "I think this is fate."

"Great. Here's part B of the fate plan. After you leave the photo session tomorrow, come back here. I'll check you out and make sure everything's good."

The next day, Jenny (wearing her new white dress and looking very sexy) had returned to Deborah Rothstein's office.

Deborah had not looked up as Jenny walked inside. The junior agent had been focused on her computer. She had clicked through a series of crisp posed shots of Jenny. The photographer had emailed Deborah the link less than an hour before.

In her tight white dress, with perfectly tousled hair ("fuck-me" hair, as Deborah and her girlfriends had called it in school), Jenny had looked simultaneously virtuous and hot. The girl exuded innocence. But there was a hint, a tantalizing *frisson*, of burning sexuality underneath.

The junior agent paused at one photo. It showed Jenny glancing into the camera with her big blue eyes, biting her lower lip. The picture captured something.

"These are good," Deborah said. "This is what I wanted."

"Are you going to explain what this is about now?"

"All right, but don't tell anyone. Promise? Okay. There is a major producer who's looking for someone who looks like you. I don't want to get your hopes up. I'm sending this producer a bunch of pictures of different girls. But if it works out, I guarantee that you will be in at least one movie before Christmas."

Jenny could not speak. Her heart raced.

"If the producer wants you, you and I will sign a contract for representation."

"So you're not my agent yet?"

"Not really. I'm hip-pocketing you as they say."

"What's hip-pocketing?"

"It means nothing, really."

"Can I tell my co-workers you've hip-pocketed me?"

"Sure, why not."

"Thank you!"

"No problem. Now get out of here. I'll call you if the producer wants you."

As she drove back to her job, Jenny had realized that she had forgotten to ask what the movie was about. Or movies. Did her hip-pocketing agent (*her agent!*) actually say "at least one movie?" As in, multiple movies?

Swag!

Three days after that, Deborah had called. "How soon can you get over here?"

Thirty minutes later in Deborah's office, Jenny had barely sat down when Deborah told her in a rush that the producer was a certain Egyptian lady, and these movies were going to be exploitation movies, and...

"Egyptian lady?" Jenny had said. "The rich one? With the big studio deal?"

"Yeah. You heard about that, huh?"

"I read the trades every day. I get the news feed on my smartphone!"

"Look at you. The producer probably sensed that there was something special about you."

"But... if I remember correctly, her movies are supposed to be arty, indie kinds of films. Not exploitation. Right?"

"We're both right. You read that news story correctly, but she has now changed her plan. You need to get ready to audition for a down and dirty exploitation movie. You don't have any problem with that, right?"

Jenny had hesitated. What would she tell her mom? And her friends? She came from a small, conservative farm community...

"Okay," Jenny had answered at last. She had nodded, trying to project confidence. "I'm in."

After scanning a contract for representation, Jenny had signed three copies and kept one. Then she and her agent got down to business.

Deborah had explained that there were no scripts yet. The producer would be asking Jenny to "extemporize."

"What's that?" the girl had asked.

"Just wing it. It won't be too hard, I promise."

"Deborah, I can't prepare without a script. What if I have to do an accent?"

"Just RELAX. That's the main thing. Look, kid, if you get too uptight about this thing, you'll blow the whole deal."

"Kid? You don't seem much older than me."

"Figure of speech. But please, just relax. You'll do fine."

Jenny had confessed her worries. "I... I really don't have much experience."

That was certainly true. Being her usual thorough self, Deborah had earlier tracked down and called the director of the lone credit on Jenny's resume, a high school production of *Godspell.*

"You want to sign *Jenny Smith?*" the school's drama teacher, a hoarse-voiced man named Marlon, had asked incredulously. "Good luck with that!"

Marlon had confirmed what Deborah had already suspected: Jenny could not act her way out of a paper bag. Plus, Jenny was particularly bad at projecting romantic chemistry with a male co-player.

"I gotta give 'er her due though," the man had added. "She is ferociously determined. I think she has the most determination to succeed of anyone I've ever met. Maybe that's enough."

"Thank you for your time."

"Are you looking for any other actors?" Marlon had asked hopefully. "I know some who can actually act…"

"Sorry, but my roster is full."

"Then why in the world are you signing Jenny Smith?"

"Like you noted, maybe that's enough," Deborah had said. "Do me a favor and keep this under your hat, okay? The last thing Jenny needs is getting jealous phone calls and emails from people back home. I need her relaxed and focused. Thank you again!"

Deborah of course had not told Jenny about the phone call. What she DID tell Jenny was that Jenny needed to wear the white dress to the audition.

Jenny had groaned. "That white dress is so tight. I can't move very well in it. What if I have to act out a scene? Hey! I have this really pretty blue dress, and it's comfortable, and it's kind of hip…"

"NO. The white dress. You promised. You said you were in."

"I am in. But this whole thing is kind of weird. The dress, the contact lenses, my new hair... I can't decide if I look more like a centerfold or a whore."

"You're supposed to look sexy. Anybody ever tell you what sexy looks like? This is an exploitation picture. Remember?"

"You're right," Jenny had admitted. "Sorry. I'm just nervous."

Deborah had turned to her computer and tapped out a quick email before hitting Send.

"I'm hoping to land a stage role soon," Jenny had added finally, trying to fill the silence. "Get some more experience... even if it's just summer stock. I'd love to play Helen of Troy. Do you think you can help me land something like that?"

"Absolutely," Deborah had mumbled as she read a reply email.

"I want to play Helen because she is strong and confident." Jenny had looked down at her shoes. "In real life, I'm kind of submissive."

"Good."

"Good?" Jenny's blue eyes had opened wide. "Why is that good?"

"Call it instinct. All right Jenny, this is it. Here we go! It's on. Show up at her office at two p.m. tomorrow. Her bungalow's in with all the other producer's cottages on the lot. She's next to Clint Eastwood. Just ask around when you arrive at the studio. You'll find it."

Jenny nodded. She looked very determined.

"And listen to me carefully. This is the most important thing." Deborah stood up and leaned across her desk, placing her fingertips on the surface in a power pose. "Anything that woman asks you to do, and I mean anything, you do it."

"Okay," Jenny had replied, her eyes opening wide once more.

And now here she was, walking across a Burbank street to the oldest and most prestigious studio in Hollywood. Her, Jenny Smith, from Woodchuck, Kansas, about to audition for a powerful producer and possibly land her first film role. It was all so amazing!

A friendly guard at the gate checked her off the scheduled-visitor list before giving her a handout map of the lot and pointing her in the right direction. Jenny arrived at the producer's bungalow exactly fifteen minutes before her appointment time, just as Deborah had instructed.

Jenny studied the cottage. It had been built during the prewar years and exuded classic and sexy film glamor.

A man strode past her, hurrying toward a sound stage. Jenny gasped. She recognized one of the most famous actors in the world. He was dressed in a plain black t-shirt and tight jeans, not looking at all like his best-known character, a comic-book hero usually outfitted in armor.

Hearing Jenny gasp, the movie star looked back over his shoulder. He grinned and winked.

Then he was gone.

I'm here, Jenny thought. *I'm really here.*

Straightening her spine, she turned and walked with purpose before knocking on the bungalow's front door.

After cooling her heels for over an hour in a walnut-paneled waiting room while trying not to fidget, Jenny was finally ushered within the inner sanctum by an annoyed-looking assistant.

As she walked in, Jenny immediately recognized the producer from the picture she had seen in *The Hollywood Reporter.*

The older woman stood up from her desk. She was dressed flawlessly in tight black couture. She radiated money, power and confidence. Studying her guest, she touched her short coif. Then she smiled. "Welcome."

"Thank you," Jenny said with a slight tremor.

The producer dismissed her assistant with a wrist-flick.

The assistant walked to the door, looked back, and curled her lip at Jenny behind Jenny's back before exiting.

"Won't you have a seat?" The producer's voice was deep and throaty. She had only the slightest trace of an Egyptian accent inside her English vowels.

Jenny obeyed, sitting and crossing her legs in a plush black leather chair that faced the desk.

"I'm tidying up a bit of business," the older woman said as she sat back down. "But I didn't want to make you wait any longer. Would you mind if I finish?"

"Of course," Jenny said. "No problem, Ms. Allegheny."

"It's Al-Anselemmy."

Jenny's button nose wrinkled in a cute perplexed expression. "Al-…"

"Why don't you just call me Houda. Everyone does."

"I'm so sorry."

"That's all right." Houda smiled before turning her attention back to papers on her desk.

As the minutes passed, Jenny's gaze wandered around the room. In addition to framed movie posters, there were gorgeous photos of exotic locations taped up here and there—beautiful waterfalls, forests, and more. Jenny stared at them. *Are those production location pictures? Are we going to be shooting in those places? That would be amazing!*

From time to time, Houda's eyes drifted up under her eyebrows. She surreptitiously studied the blonde girl. *So lovely,* she thought. *Oh, she is perfect.* Houda looked back down and frowned. *Deborah drove a hard bargain. The price is high.* After another moment, the older woman made up her mind. *But the girl is worth it.*

Jenny turned as her potential employer spoke to her: "What did Deborah tell you about your audition today?"

"Not much," Jenny admitted. "She said that I

should just relax. And that I would have to wing it, you know, extemporize whatever direction you might give me for a scene."

"That's exactly right." The older woman leaned back and touched her chin. "Why don't we begin by letting me take a look at you?"

Jenny stood up. *Relax, right?* she thought. *Okay, I can do that.* She smiled and pirouetted playfully, lifting one foot like a ballerina. Her long blonde hair flowed around her shoulders.

"Hmm," Houda said, trying not to betray her mounting excitement. "I don't know."

Jenny's face fell. "No. Wait! Here." The girl walked back and forth across the room.

The Egyptian studied the pert butt moving underneath the tight white fabric. "Not bad," she said. "But I still don't know."

"But you haven't seen me act!"

"Eh."

"I can do whatever you want me to do," Jenny said with total confidence. "I can recite... Oh. I was going to say, I can recite a speech from *The Tempest*. But this is an exploitation picture, huh?"

"Indeed. In fact, there are three."

"Three!"

"I'm not sure which one you might be good for. Would you like to audition for them all?"

"Would I!"

Houda smiled. "I don't know. Maybe I need to think about it. Perhaps you should come back some other time."

Jenny thought wildly. "Deborah told me to wear some see-through lingerie under my dress. She said you might need to take a look at my body, to see if I was the right physical type."

"I suppose we could. But first, why don't you lock the door. And would you mind closing the window blinds? We want to preserve your privacy, after all."

"Sure, I would be happy to."

As Jenny performed the privacy measures, Houda pressed an intercom button and told her assistant: no interruptions. Houda hung up before the assistant could grumble a reply.

The older woman rose from her office chair and walked around her desk. She effortlessly lifted the heavy plush leather chair that Jenny had been sitting in and turned it around so that it faced the open middle of the room.

Gee she's strong, Jenny thought with surprise. Houda had already impressed her with her charisma, a vibration of power. *I guess she's just all-around strong and powerful.*

Houda sat in the leather, striking a naturally elegant pose. After a moment, she lifted her eyebrows at Jenny.

Oh, Jenny thought. *Right!* The blonde managed to unzip the back of her white dress. She pulled it up and over her body and threw it onto a coffee table. Kicking her flats under the table as well, Jenny was suddenly clad only in a matching red lace bra and panties.

The older woman frowned. "Come closer."

Jenny obeyed. She approached as close as she dared, almost touching the older woman's knee with her bare leg.

"Your skin is so pale," Houda murmured. She touched Jenny's stomach, her finger drawing a slow journey down.

"Yeah," Jenny said, groaning. "It's the bane of my life. But don't worry, I'm sure if I go to a tanning salon I can get darker."

"As dark as me?" the older woman asked playfully. She let her whole arm touch Jenny's torso, highlighting the contrast between her Arab pigmentation and Jenny's fair skin.

Jenny laughed. "I wish I was as dark as you. I hate being so white. It's totally boring."

"Your underwear," Houda said. She slipped a fingernail into the lace waistband of Jenny's panties. "It doesn't fit properly. It's a bit tight, don't you think?"

"I'm sorry," Jenny gasped. "Deborah just told me about the lingerie thing this morning. This stuff was the best I could find at the department store on short notice. I know it sucks."

"Yes, it does indeed suck." The older woman pulled the elastic material out to its limit before letting it snap back onto the girl's skin.

"I'm sorry," Jenny repeated, trying not to wince with the sting. "Do you want me to take it off?"

A long pause followed.

"I have a better idea."

Puzzled, Jenny watched Houda sit back and withdraw her phone from her pocket. "The first movie is about a stripper," the producer said, smiling. "She becomes entangled with a crime syndicate. They kidnap her sister. They are going to kill the sister. So the stripper goes to see the kingpin. Do you follow me?"

"I think so…"

"Alone, with the kingpin, in his office, the stripper strips for him. She must seduce him to make him fall in love with her and let her sister go. And so she performs the striptease of her life. It is sexy, visceral, amazing."

Jenny nodded excitedly. "I work out with online Strippercize videos. I could totally do that!"

"Mmn. Perhaps. I don't know. I need to be convinced. Are you sure you could seduce a hard mafia gangster?"

"I totally could. If my sister's life was on the line, I totally could. I don't actually have a sister, in reality. But you know what I mean."

Houda smiled. She thumbed her phone. Prince's *Gett Off* began playing out of it. The older woman placed the phone on the hardwood floor next to the chair, setting it upright. She then sat back once more and crossed her legs, waiting.

Look at her, Jenny thought. *She is so strong and confident and powerful. I've never met anyone like Houda. It won't be hard to imagine her as Tony Soprano.* She shook her head, dismissing her reverie as she tried to get into character. *Good! Use that vibe she has. Make it work for you. Method.*

"Your sister ain't going nowhere," the older woman said in a deep gruff voice.

In response, Jenny began gyrating her hips in a slow sexy circle. She pushed her fingers up into her hair.

The woman in black shook her head. No dice.

Oh yeah? Jenny bent forward, placing her hands on the arms of the chair, inches from Houda's own. She arched her back, doing a slow belly-dance.

Houda looked unimpressed.

Jenny whipped her hair up over her head, letting it fall all over the Egyptian woman's face. She nuzzled her own face into the crook of Houda's neck. Jenny heard the producer breathe in, inhaling scent as the silky blonde hair slid down.

The girl whipped her hair back over her shoulders, straightening. Locking her gaze with the powerful woman's smoky dark eyes, Jenny slowly reached behind her back.

Despite herself, Houda smiled.

"Please," Jenny said in a small voice. "Please let my sister go."

The red lace bra fell to the floor.

The producer shrugged. She glanced at the covered window, as if looking for something more interesting.

Jenny slid her hands up her torso. Cupping her breasts, she began massaging them, slowly. *I'm actually getting turned on,* Jenny thought. *Good! Use that! Method! This mafia guy is going to kill your sister. Seduce him!*

Bending forward once more, Jenny lowered her milky breasts, caressing them, until they were almost touching the older woman's face. Reluctantly, Houda's eyes drifted back to the show. The blonde girl rubbed her thumbs over her pale nipples, hardening them into pebbles.

"I dunno," Houda said. It wasn't clear if the gangster was speaking, or her.

Jenny turned around, dancing. "I'll do anything," she said. And it was not clear if the stripper was speaking, or Jenny.

The blonde backed up, gyrating with the beat, until her butt was almost touching the older woman's face. Jenny hooked her fingers into the waistband of her lace panties and peeled the fabric down slowly, revealing her perfect ass millimeter by millimeter.

Houda flicked out her tongue playfully.

Jenny shrieked, giggled, and said: "Hey! No fair, you can't make me break character!"

"All kinds of things happen on the set, my dear," the older woman murmured, watching the girl's exquisite bottom expose itself. "You must show me you can maintain focus."

Jenny closed her eyes, concentrating on the sexy music as she maintained a slow steady stripper gyration. As if in a trance, she finally let her red lace panties slide down her long legs to the floor.

She felt Houda's hands touch her butt ever so lightly. Then they began to caress, massaging her firm flesh. *Is this part of the script?* Jenny wondered. *Or is Houda letting me know that I passed the test and the gangster fell for me?* Either way, Jenny concluded that the audition was going exceedingly well.

"Very good, my dear," the older woman said. She planted a long slow kiss on both of Jenny's quivering cheeks, letting her lips linger. "We Egyptians are passionate people, and that is why I kiss you."

Following Houda's instructions, Jenny stopped dancing and sat on the arm of the chair. The producer turned off the music and draped Jenny's arms around her neck before letting her own hands wander over the girl's body.

"How did I do?" Jenny asked.

"Not too bad."

"That's good, right?"

"Yes."

"Yay!"

The woman smiled. She snaked one arm around Jenny, pulling her tight.

"You're really strong," Jenny said.

"I am a Crossfit champion."

"What's Crossfit?"

"It's like the gym."

"Oh."

Jenny closed her eyes, enjoying the feel of the strong woman holding her close. After a moment she laid her head on Houda's shoulder. She sighed. She felt safe.

"Perhaps you are tired," the producer murmured, kissing her blonde head.

"No, I'm fine. I'm ready for another audition. If you want me to."

The second film, Houda explained, was about a girl who came to terms with her need for BDSM.

"Oh, kind of like *Fifty Shades of Grey?*"

"Yes, exactly." The producer smiled, lightly massaging Jenny's naked body here and there.

"I read that book," Jenny said. "It really turned me on."

"It did?"

"Yeah." Jenny hesitated, then dropped her eyes. She looked vulnerable. "I've wondered sometimes, more often than I would like to admit actually, what all that kind of stuff is like—you know, in the book and in the movie. I've never done anything like that."

"I see."

"You must think I'm a total psycho," Jenny said, her voice catching. She seemed close to tears.

"Not at all."

"This is so weird, like, I just feel—*comfortable* with you. I feel like I can tell you anything. And I swear I'm not trying to play up to you for a role or whatever. I'm being real."

"I believe you. Why don't we try something? In this second movie, there is a scene where the heroine is spanked for the first time."

Jenny's eyes grew wide.

"And," Houda continued, "she discovers a kind of pleasure in it. Ecstasy."

"Oh my God," Jenny breathed. "It's like *Secretary*. With Maggie Gyllenhaal and James Spader!"

"Quite, yes. You're very good."

"I love that movie! I have never told anyone that before."

"I love it too. Now why don't we get up."

As they both rose to their feet, Jenny asked: "Are all your movies, well, do they all have women lead characters?"

"Yes," Houda said as she retrieved an expensive leather satchel near the wall. She set it upon her desk.

"Wow. That's really amazing. *You're* amazing. I've never met anyone like you."

"Thank you. Now here."

Jenny looked down. Houda was holding out a pair of handcuffs that she had withdrawn from the satchel.

"What's that?"

"I brought a few things for the audition today."

"Oh."

"Perhaps you are having second thoughts?"

"No!" Jenny took the cuffs.

In short order, Jenny was lowering her naked body face-down onto Houda's lap, on the couch.

"Should I put the cuffs on now?" Jenny asked after she had arranged herself. She glanced at an antique gilt-edged mirror facing her on the opposite wall. In the reflection she saw Houda smiling and staring at her heart-shaped butt.

"No," Houda said. "I have changed my mind." The older woman took the cuffs from Jenny and threw them backward over her shoulder. They landed with a crash somewhere on the hardwood floor.

"Oh," Jenny said uncertainly. Did that mean no spanking? She felt suddenly, bitterly disappointed.

"Keep your hands by your sides," Houda said. "But by no means cover your derrière."

"My what?"

"Your ass."

"Oh."

"This is about discipline. I must see how strong your self-control is."

"Wow. Okay. But, I thought this scene was in the movie?"

"It is."

Jenny thought.

"Can I ask a question before we begin?" she finally asked. Houda's fingers were tracing the curves and borders of her beautiful rump.

"Yes."

"Thank you. So, who am I? What's my character? What's my motivation?"

"This person is you, Jenny. Whatever you feel, the character feels. Whatever you want, the character wants."

It blew Jenny's mind. "So. Uh. Then, like, in the script, how can I play myself if the writer obviously hasn't met me?"

"The script hasn't been written yet."

"Really?"

Houda leaned sideways and kissed between Jenny's shoulder blades. She slipped her fingers between the girl's butt cheeks, making Jenny gasp. "Are you ready?"

"Yeah," Jenny whispered.

Houda's fingers slid in and out between Jenny's firm white cheeks… slowly. After a while, Jenny thought: *This doesn't hurt at all.* She looked at the mirror again and saw that her pretty face had flushed bright red. *Wow. This is crazy!*

Then the older woman's strong hand lifted and came down squarely on the round of one cheek: CRACK!

Jenny gasped. "Ow! Ow, ow, ow, owwww…" she sang, the note rising higher and higher.

Houda's hand massaged the spot where it had hit. A strange heat began invading Jenny's body. It made her feel funny.

Then her other butt-cheek felt the slap: CRACK!

"Agh!" Jenny huffed. Her eyes bugged out as

her entire body arched backward into a crescent. "Oh, God. Oh, wow."

"What did you say?"

"Uh. I said… Oh, ow," Jenny lied. "Ow. Ow. Oh, it hurts."

And it did hurt. But there was something else—a deep kind of *rich* feeling that she could not describe in words but that she would think about for many, many days to come.

Houda continued to spank her, more lightly. She peppered the girl's ass expertly, covering the entire beautiful hill with a stinging palm.

"Ow," Jenny groaned.

Suddenly all the strength went out of her. Jenny's bones collapsed, like a marionette whose strings had been cut. Nothing like this had ever happened to her before. *I have totally lost control of my body,* her brain registered dimly.

As if realizing the girl's helplessness, Houda whispered: "I think that's enough now." She began rubbing her ass tenderly, moving down the legs and up the back, helping to seep her own strength into Jenny's muscles.

Jenny breathed hard. Blonde hair was plastered all over her sweaty face. A little bit of drool had pooled on the leather where her cheek was pressed into the cushion.

"You have done very well, my dear," Houda said. "I think we should postpone the rest of our audition, yes? I do not believe you can continue."

"No!" Jenny struggled upright. Her boobs

bounced and jiggled. Houda tried to help her. Somehow, Jenny wound up straddling Houda.

"I hope I don't stain your nice dress," Jenny said. She glanced down. The golden thatch between her thighs had become unaccountably wet.

"That's all right, my dear," the older woman said. She smiled and placed Jenny's arms once more around her neck before massaging the girl's ass.

"I can audition some more," Jenny said. "There are three movies, right? I've done two. What's the third?"

"A beautiful young spy. She is captured and tortured by terrorists. They try to break her to reveal the secret. But she does not give in."

"Wow."

"Yes."

"I've always wanted to play a spy. I love James Bond. Not the James Bond girls, but the guy. I've always thought there should be a kind of James Bond girl-spy."

Houda looked at Jenny's perfect boobs, rising and falling with every breath Jenny took. The older woman grinned and slid her hands up to knead the breasts, sliding her thumbs over the nipples, making headlights. "That's exactly what this is. If the first film does well, it may even turn into a series franchise."

"No way! A tentpole? That's what they call it, right? A series that makes big money?"

"Yes. You're very smart."

"Thank you." Jenny smiled down at the older woman, who smiled back. Jenny wanted to grind her hips on Houda's lap, but resisted the urge. It didn't seem professional.

"So," the producer said. "Why don't we get up. You may go stand under that ceiling fan over there."

Soon Jenny was waiting under a motionless big brass ceiling fan that looked like it was left over from World War II. She gazed up at it uncertainly. *What now?*

"Here," Houda said as she tossed over a length of soft rope that she had retrieved from the satchel. Jenny only just managed to catch it in time. "Loop it over the fan," Houda continued, "and make it secure so that it won't come off. Your hands will be cuffed high to the rope, if I can find wherever it is that I threw those handcuffs."

"Is this safe?" Jenny looked up with a doubtful expression. "It looks super heavy."

"Then it must be secured very strongly if it's so heavy. Don't worry."

The naked girl tied an acceptable harness, knotting a loop high over her head.

"And here are the handcuffs," Houda said, holding them up as she approached. "I looked under every piece of furniture, and of course it was the last one."

"Great. I'm really excited!"

"You are so positive. I must say, just like you said earlier that you have never met anyone like me? I have never met anyone like you, either."

"Wow. Thank you. That really means a lot to me. Sincerely."

"You're welcome. Now in order to do this scene, I should probably disrobe also."

"What? Why?"

With a smile, Houda pointed to a wet patch on her skirt just under her stomach. It was where Jenny's golden bush had been resting when the girl had been straddling her.

"God, I am so sorry," Jenny stuttered. "I will totally pay the dry cleaning bill."

"Not to worry my dear."

"I just don't know what happened to me, back then…"

"Enough! Don't give it another thought. But I think in the interest of prudence, I will take off my clothes. Unless you object?"

"No of course not, Ms. Al-… Ms. Houda. I don't mind at all."

Jenny caught the handcuffs that Houda tossed to her. The blonde cuffed her wrists inside the high loop of rope, making sure that the fan was indeed strong enough to hold her weight. It was, to spare.

Arms high, Jenny then watched the older woman undress. The producer folded each item of her clothing unhurriedly before setting it upon the coffee table where Jenny's white dress still lay flung.

Houda was not beautiful in a conventional sense, but her dark body appeared fit and healthy and perfectly toned. Her small breasts gave her a runner's physique. She looked younger than her years. The only area of her body that appeared uncontrolled was a patch of black hair between her thighs that grew wild and untrimmed. Jenny noted with surprise that Houda's pubic hair, like her own, was wet.

The blonde glanced over her shoulder at the antique wall mirror behind her. Jenny saw that her butt was still glowing a nice rosy red. *It looks beautiful,* she thought.

"Perhaps you can come visit me at my vacation home in Curaçao," Houda murmured as she slid her fingers up and down Jenny's body for the umpteenth time.

"Uh," Jenny said, turning back to face her interrogator. She tried to focus. "Where?"

"Curaçao."

"What's that?"

"It is the loveliest island on earth."

"Oh." Jenny sighed. Houda's hands felt so good. "Yes. That sounds nice."

"It is only appropriate… because you are the loveliest girl on earth."

Jenny blushed deeply. She smiled at the floor.

Houda arranged stray blonde locks on Jenny's face. "My house is on the beach. The waves at night, in the moonlight… I want to show them to you."

It sounds amazing, Jenny thought. "Oh yes, Ms.... Houda. I would love to come and visit you at your beautiful waterfront home."

"Good."

"But," Jenny said with great determination, "I want to show you that I can do this role. I can do any role."

"Very well. I am the evil terrorist leader. You must not give in to me."

"Oh. Okay! You're, like, the Ayatollah!"

"Um, no. Oh, all right. Fine. Whatever. Yes, the Ayatollah." The older woman made an impatient sound, staring at Jenny's young lush pale naked body.

"Has this script been written, either?"

"Not yet. And now, stop asking so many questions! Get into character."

Jenny's eyes closed. Then they popped open, with a hint of lunacy. "I will never give in to you, Ayatollah! You can forget it!"

"Silly girl," Houda hissed in a menacing bass rumble. "You do not yet know your peril."

"No!" Jenny thrashed violently, putting on a show. The massive ceiling fan didn't budge. "Never!"

The older woman reached behind Jenny's ear and seized a nape of blonde hair. She crushed her mouth upon Jenny's, forcing her tongue inside.

"MMMmmmmmnnnn," Jenny moaned. Her thrashing turned into a writhing.

Houda's hand closed hard upon Jenny's breast, pinching her delicate nipple painfully between thumb and forefinger. The producer broke off the kiss and began sliding her teeth down the blonde girl's neck.

"Oh my God," Jenny moaned. "I won't. I can't. I will never give in… there's no way…"

When her mouth had reached the area just below Jenny's clavicle, Houda sucked a mouthful of white skin, hard. She then ripped her mouth away, leaving a bright red hickey on the middle of the girl's chest.

"Ow," Jenny said. "Wow. Ow. Ow, ow, no. There is no way. You can just give up, Ayatollah. I will never give in to youuuUUUUUuuuu oh my God…"

The girl had reacted to Houda's fingers, pushed between her legs into the blonde curls, slipping expertly. Houda moaned and turned the girl's body slightly so that the older woman could rub her own bush against Jenny. She pulled Jenny's trembling knee up between her own legs.

"No way," Jenny gasped. "God, Ayatollah… I can't…"

The older woman slurped and bit each of Jenny's breasts, making the girl gasp louder.

Jenny felt her body beginning to buzz, the sign of approaching orgasm. Houda intuited Jenny's vibrations and began synchronizing her movements to Jenny's writhing. "Never," Jenny whispered as if in a trance, her eyes closed. "I won't... You can't..."

Houda orchestrated Jenny's body expertly, bringing the girl closer and closer to orgasm, as if manipulating the waves of the ocean to swell higher and higher without quite breaking, not yet.

"Oh," Jenny sniffled in a heartbreaking voice. She coughed. "Oh no. No, a thousand times no..."

"Oh yes, my dear," Houda said, kneeling before her captive and throwing the girl's thighs roughly over her shoulders. Her strong hands clamped upon Jenny's butt so that she couldn't wiggle away. "Now tilt your hips up so I can better eat that pretty pussy of yours."

Jenny's eyes snapped open. "Wha'... What..."

She looked down. Houda was holding her up. The older woman's eyes were closed as her lips moved up and down through Jenny's golden pubic hair, eating her hard.

"Oh my God," Jenny said in a tone that she had never used before in her life. "Ms. Houda... I mean, Ayatollah... you can't... this isn't... oh... oh, my God..."

Once again, Jenny lost control of her body. Her hips tilted themselves up so that the strong older woman could indeed eat her pussy as much as she wanted. Then Jenny's ankles locked themselves behind Houda's neck. *Is this really happening?* some dim part of Jenny's brain wondered. She heard the sound of an approaching train. *Wow that's loud,* Jenny thought in the same surreal way. *They must be shooting a crazy kind of movie around here.* And then, as the orgasm hit her, her blue eyes rolled into the back of her head and she realized that the sound had been coming from her.

Jenny's spasms finally ceased. She hung from the handcuffs as limp as spaghetti over a fork.

Houda reluctantly pulled her mouth away from the girl's burning bush, staring at the slippery blonde curls. She then gave a few more kisses and licks for good measure, moaning. Jenny jumped but made no sound.

The older woman stood slowly. She unlocked the handcuffs and placed Jenny's arm gently around her strong shoulders, holding the girl up. "Careful now," Houda murmured into her ear. "Don't fall."

Jenny did not reply. Her eyes were closed. Only her chest moved, still breathing heavily.

The girl allowed Houda to half-carry her, like a child, back to the couch. The Egyptian woman tenderly placed Jenny onto the leather cushions, face-down. She kissed the blonde girl's sweaty face. "We are not done yet, Jenny," Houda said.

Jenny's eyelids fluttered slightly at Houda's first speaking of her name.

Through her haze, the blonde watched the older woman walk with her usual confident stroll to the satchel on the desk. Jenny's eyes closed again. She fell asleep.

She awoke shortly after to the feeling of being

moved. Houda was raising her butt in the air.

Dragging her face across the leather cushion to look over her shoulder, Jenny saw Houda buckling a cruelly large black strapon. Houda smiled at the girl. "This is the part where the spy has to take it, Jenny. Are you ready?"

With a barely perceptible movement, Jenny nodded.

"Then raise your ass higher, arch your back, and hold on to the couch."

The girl obeyed. She felt like she was in a dream. Nothing seemed real. Houda was holding her hips, stroking her gently between her legs... so gently...

And then, Jenny felt it. Going in. Slowly.

"Ohhhhhh," she said, gripping the cushions harder. "Oh, God. Houda."

"Yes my darling," Houda whispered. "Say my name."

"Houda."

"Louder." The older woman began moving her pelvis back and forth, holding Jenny's waist immobile.

"Houda," Jenny cried. "Houuudaaaaa. Oh God, Houuuudaaaaaa."

Jenny moaned louder and louder as the older woman's movements grew faster and rougher. Houda slipped her hand down over Jenny's stomach between her legs, rubbing her clitoris while maintaining a thrusting rhythm. "I want you to come again, Jenny," she hissed. "Come for me my sweet."

"Oh God, yes. Oh. OH."

Without warning, Jenny's sweaty body began jerking and convulsing, nearly making her capsize off the couch. "Ohhhh... Ohhhh... Houda... God..."

When Jenny's orgasm had passed, the older woman drew the phallus slowly from the girl. Houda watched the black dildo slide out through the golden hair.

"Ow," Jenny whispered in a voice so low and soft it almost was not spoken at all.

"My darling," Houda murmured. She settled herself low so that she could kiss Jenny's aching vagina. Soft kisses, full of tenderness, her lips and tongue offering a healing touch.

With her last remaining bit of energy, Jenny moved one hand back. She interlaced her fingers with Houda as the older woman gently used her mouth, soothing her.

Later, Jenny did not remember how long they had lain there like that. But of everything she had experienced that day, afterward she thought about that the most.

Finally, Houda stood and dressed herself, unfolding her clothes before putting them on once again. Then she turned to the nearly comatose naked girl on the couch. "Come now."

Jenny allowed Houda to slip the red lace panties back upon her, and clip the bra behind her back. Then Houda took the girl by both hands, raising her to her feet. In a daze, Jenny watched more than felt the older woman lowering the white dress over her before zipping up the back, taking care not to let any of Jenny's hair spill into the zipper.

Houda looked at her with warm eyes. "Can you walk?"

"I think so," Jenny said through her fog.

At the door, Houda took Jenny in a tender embrace. She held her.

After a moment, Jenny returned the hug, setting her head on the older woman's shoulder.

At length Houda took a step back. Her eyes were moist. "Jenny, I cannot contact you again until the movies are finished. That was part of the deal. I don't even have your phone number, email, anything. I could ask you for it but I am an honorable woman. You may not understand right now."

Jenny did not understand much of anything, at present. Her brain was not working too well.

Houda spoke with a fierce intensity, staring into the girl's dazed blue eyes. "I have been waiting all my life for someone like you. It may be too much to hope that you will return my feelings. But, Jenny, I promise you: if you choose the love I will offer you, there will be only you for me."

On her drive home, Jenny tried to remember what Houda had said. A life... together? What? She, Jenny, had just been ravished on the casting couch, quite literally. And her body was still vibrating. It felt like a tuning fork that would not stop humming.

I bet there aren't even going to be any movies, Jenny thought.

She was wrong. Over the next six months, Houda's production company shot three films in quick succession. They were all adaptations of arty novels that had sold middling-to-very-well in bookstores. All of the movies had female protagonists. But the films certainly weren't exploitation pictures, unless the books' authors perhaps felt exploited by the liberties the studio took in the screen adaptations.

In each film, Jenny had been cast. But not as the lead, or even as a principal; instead, Jenny had had bit parts. Her only speaking role had been in the last one, where she had actually played a barista. Her one line had been when Jenny had asked her customer, the star: "Would you like foam?"

Somebody told her the part had been specially written and inserted into the script.

"You just don't have enough acting experience yet, honey," Deborah said during one of Jenny's visits to her office. "But don't worry, you're gonna get better."

"Sure. Sure I am." The girl watched movers carry furniture out. Deborah had just made full agent. Senior management had given her a bigger office, a corner office in fact.

Jenny's agent regarded her. "Listen," Deborah said. "True story, no bullshit. If anybody had told me back in the day that Matthew McConaughey would be an Oscar winner AND box office A-list, I would've told them to get their crack out of my face. The guy sucked. He stank. He was a stupid dumb hick from Texas with a redneck accent and his acting was even worse than yours, no offense."

Jenny stared. "Deborah, you're so young. What do you mean, 'back in the day?'"

Deborah named her agency's archrival, a percentery across town. "My dad's the head."

"No way."

"I'm surprised you haven't heard. Anyway, I used to hang around all these actors when I was growing up. And I heard all the stories. I've heard everything. And I'm telling you, for real, as honestly as a talent agent can open her mouth: what set Matthew McConaughey apart was sheer ambition and a capacity for extremely hard work. That's what you've got also. McConaughey wasn't born good. He got good. You can too. That's it. That's my pep talk, kid."

"I wish you would stop calling me kid."

"Take it as a compliment. Have you ever heard of Robert Evans? An incredibly great producer. He wrote a book. It's called *The Kid Stays In The Picture*. So maybe every time I call you kid, you will remind yourself: stay in the picture. Stay in this industry. You're sexy like McConaughey. If he can do it, you can. You can be a star, no kidding."

Then Deborah's expression changed. She looked like she was, perhaps for the first time in her life, feeling guilty. "What happened that day? When you went to Houda's office?"

Jenny cocked her head. "Why don't you ask Houda?"

"Maybe I did."

"No you didn't."

"You're right, I didn't. I'm a little scared of her. She's an extremely powerful lady."

Jenny looked down. "I know."

"So, c'mon," Deborah asked in a confidential tone. "What happened?"

"We talked. She said you had some good actors, who she was probably going to cast in the leads of her upcoming movies. And of course that's what happened."

"Not all of the actors were mine. She used some other agencies."

"Two out of the three leads were your clients. And four of the principals."

"Yes," Deborah admitted. "So, nothing happened?"

"Was something supposed to happen?"

Deborah studied her client carefully. "I think you may be smarter than I thought. And that means maybe you're going to have a good career in this town."

Jenny said nothing.

Deborah raised her hands. "Okay. I'll never mention it again. But listen, I'm your agent as long as you want me."

The blonde smiled. "Good. I have a feeling that YOU are going to have a GREAT career in this town."

As Jenny was leaving, she paused and looked back. "Has Houda's third movie wrapped yet?"

"Why? Want to see your dailies? I can get them."

"Sure… but just wondering when the last movie will be done."

"Two more weeks. Oh, by the way: here."

Jenny accepted an envelope. "What's this?"

"A plane ticket and a program. Some repertory company is putting *Helen of Troy* on stage next month. Since you will have three movie credits soon, I was able to convince them to cast you. Convincing them to pay for your airfare was tougher, but I love a challenge. Four weeks in Wisconsin: two rehearsal, two production. Send me a postcard."

That weekend, Jenny went alone to the beach in Santa Monica.

The following Monday, she called Deborah.

"Hey kid," said the agent. "What's up?"

"I want to talk to Houda."

"Whoa."

"You heard me. And don't ask why. It's private."

"Uh-huh. Are you feeling all right? Have you

been drinking or doing any drugs?"

"No. I want to talk to Houda. Give me her number."

"Jenny, it's not that simple."

The girl took a deep breath. "Why?"

"Because in order to call Houda I need a really, really good reason."

"You want a reason?" Jenny shouted. "Then how about this? I wasn't the same person when I walked out of her office as when I walked in. She changed me. It scared me at first. I went through all kinds of crazy stuff—you wouldn't believe the thoughts that have been going through my head these past months."

"Whoa," Deborah repeated.

"But I went to the beach, and I stared at the water for a long time, and I realized I want to see the waves in the moonlight in Curaçao."

"Curaçao? The drink?"

"No. It's an island. The most beautiful island on earth."

"You're losing me here."

"Houda's number. What is it?"

The agent expelled a long, drawn-out sigh. "Okay. But you're going to have to wait nine more days."

"WHY?"

"Because that was the deal. No more contact between you two until all the movies are in the can."

"Fine. I don't understand, but fine. That's

what Houda said, too."

"When you two had your really boring conversation in her office?"

"I'm ignoring that. Nine more days. So, next Wednesday?"

"Yep."

"I can always just walk back into her office, you know."

"Yeah. You can sneak through studio security and hope you don't get arrested. But a beautiful, sexy girl like you tends to draw attention. Besides, if Houda herself told you the deal, why would she break it now, this close to being done?"

Jenny stewed.

"Talk to me a week from Wednesday." Deborah hung up.

On the day, early, Jenny strode into her agent's office. It was considerably bigger than the old one.

"Speak of the devil," Deborah said into her office phone. "She just walked in. May I put you on hold, please?" She pressed a button, laid the phone on her desk, and rose to her feet. She pointed at the receiver. "Houda."

"Are you kidding?"

"How many times have I kidded around with you?" Deborah walked past the blonde girl. "I'll give you some privacy. Talk as long as you want. I need to do some walking-around chatting anyway. The animals in this place, you have to look into their eyes to get the truth. And even then, fifty-

fifty." Deborah pulled the door shut as she exited.

Jenny stared at the phone. Its red hold button was blinking.

She hurried around the desk and sat in Deborah's chair. Picking up the receiver, she said: "Houda?"

No response. "Hello?"

Duuuuh, she thought. Her finger punched the hold button. The light stopped flashing. "Hello?"

"Jenny?" The husky English accent tinged with exoticism had never sounded so welcome.

"Hi Houda."

"It is so nice to hear your voice."

"I was thinking the exact same thing."

A long silence followed.

"I don't know how much you know about the deal," Houda said finally. "But I never expected…"

"I don't want to know about the deal," Jenny interrupted. "I don't care."

"I was not the same person when you left that day as when you arrived," the older woman said softly. "You changed me."

Jenny said nothing, but breathed harder.

"Do you want to… talk?" Houda asked.

"In Curaçao? I'd love to."

Houda laughed. "I'd love to, as well. But unfortunately this movie business seems to be consuming me. My films are in post-production. And there will be more… but I promise you, the two of us can get away, soon."

"When can I see you?" Jenny asked.

"Tonight."

"At your office?"

"My house would be better. It's more comfortable."

"I'd like that."

Jenny wrote down an address in Bel-Air, repeating it back. She also remembered to exchange phone numbers.

"So, a question," the older woman said. "And please forgive me, I'm accustomed to the hardness of the world. But do you want to talk to me because you're interested in another role?"

"I'm interested… in you."

"I had to ask."

"I know."

"Eight o'clock. Will that work?"

"Yes."

"I will have food if you're hungry."

They said their goodbyes. Houda hung up first, then Jenny. The girl pushed the scrap of paper with the address and phone number deep down into her pocket before she stood up.

Reaching for the door handle, she paused. In one of Deborah's shiny bookcases the spine of a book, nested among many scripts, read: *The Kid Stays In The Picture*.

Jenny pulled out the book and looked at it. Then she opened the door and walked out, taking the book with her.

THE END

Thanks for reading! If you have time, please review *Audition*. I read every review, and I appreciate honest feedback!

If you enjoyed this book, you may also enjoy

The Beard

By Anne Eton

When tall, pretty Kelly interviews at Washington D.C.'s premier LGBT-centric lobbying firm, she claims she has a girlfriend. Nothing could be further from the truth; she's never even kissed a girl. Kelly's hired. However, a suspicious co-worker keeps inquiring about her girlfriend. To keep her lies straight, Kelly bases her fictional partner on Anna, an aggressive, gorgeous lesbian friend of a friend. But when the firm's annual Christmas party looms, Kelly's forced to produce her mysterious girlfriend. The real Anna agrees to be Kelly's "beard"—her fake date. But at the party, alcohol flows… and Anna's all over Kelly. Kelly pretends to her office mates that her "girlfriend's" advances are perfectly normal—even as she feels her resistance to the beautiful woman melting away.

The Beard is a comedy with sexy scenes and some explicit passages.

Excerpt follows!

The Beard

Excerpt:

Kelly stumbled, tipsy. Anna guided her with a sure hand to the office supply room, opening the door and escorting her inside.

"Hey! Office supplies," Kelly said with false cheer. She looked around nervously. "You need some gel pens? Ha, ha!"

Anna smirked. She shut the door behind them and pressed the doorknob's button, locking it.

"Or paper clips, or toner," Kelly babbled, casually backing away. "It's a regular Staples in here!"

"Yes," Anna replied. The blonde gave Anna a sexy look and flipped a wall switch. The room went dark.

"I think we should talk about expectations," Kelly said in the pitch black, as if discussing the price of a car. "I admit, I did sort of use you for my own ends…"

"Yes."

Kelly felt Anna's hands. The tall girl backed away; she came up against waist-high pallets of paper boxes.

"You see," Kelly gasped, "I know we're supposed to be pretending that you're my girlfriend—"

"Yes... yes..." Anna murmured. She began slipping Kelly's dress up as the taller girl moved awkwardly against the immovable cartons.

Also by Anne Eton

ABOUT THE AUTHOR

I write first-time F/F erotic romance. I love what I do!

If you would like to know when I publish new books, please join my New Release Mailing List, at my site! I don't share my readers' email with anyone, for any reason.

www.anneeton.com

Thanks for reading!

Anne

www.ingramcontent.com/pod-product-compliance
Lightning Source LLC
Chambersburg PA
CBHW071316200626
46813CB00015B/2237